Gabby Dawnay

Alex Barrow

If I had a dinosaur

 Thames & Hudson

I do like

I've got a

A  is far too wet.

Because you see, I really want a different sort of pet.

I thought about a

I thought about a

But I want a pet much bigger,
more the size of, well,

A HOUSE!

I really want a giant pet, enormous, big and strong, with a body broad and solid, and a tail that's super long.

Oh if I had a **DINOSAUR**

I'd teach him lots of tricks,
like how to roll and how to sit
and fetch and carry sticks!

If I had a dinosaur, I'd walk him in the park.

I wonder if my dinosaur would roar?

Or would he bark?

If I had a dinosaur, he'd carry me to school
and all my friends would shout, 'Oh wow!

Your dinosaur is cool!'

My dinosaur would learn to count and say the alphabet ...

... and all the teachers would declare,

'Why,
what a clever pet!'

Dinosaurs need water
(I think they like to swim)

I'd have to dig a massive pond
and fill it to the brim.

If I had a dinosaur,
I'd feed him lots of greens,
like cabbages and broccoli
to keep him full of beans!

Dinosaurs make smashing pets,
as dinosaurs can do
much better stuff than dogs or cats.

Just watch out for the ...

If I had a dinosaur,
I'd get a 'dino-flap',

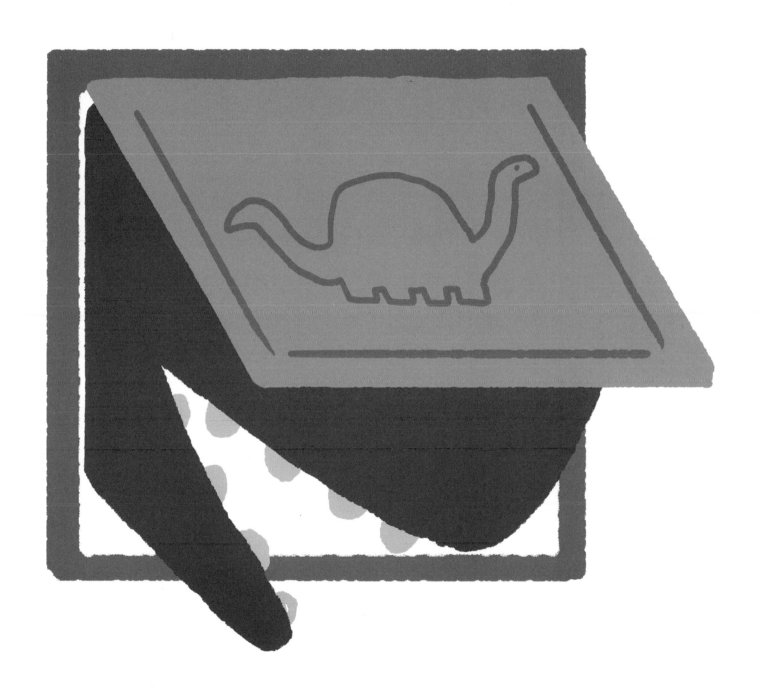

so he could come inside my house
and take a little nap.

Our sofa is enormous,
it's big enough for four.
Just perfect for a sleepy sort
of friendly dinosaur.

I wish I had a dinosaur,
to cuddle up at night,
to read a bedtime story with
and give my dad a fright!

Yes, dinosaurs make awesome pets,
I'm sure you will agree
that of all the pets they are the best –
just get one and you'll see!

For Mimi, Olla, Kip and Frank - G. D.

For my son Kasper - A. B.

With thanks to Sir David Attenborough, whose BBC documentary *Attenborough and the Giant Dinosaur* brought this enormous discovery to life.

First published in the United Kingdom in 2017 by
Thames & Hudson Ltd, 181A High Holborn, London WC1V 7QX

First paperback edition 2018

If I had a dinosaur © 2017 Thames & Hudson Ltd, London

British Library Cataloguing-in-Publication Data
A catalogue record for this book is available from the British Library

ISBN 978-0-500-65150-6

Printed and bound in China by Everbest Printing Co. Ltd

To find out about all our publications, please visit
www.thamesandhudson.com. There you can
subscribe to our e-newsletter, browse or download
our current catalogue, and buy any titles that are in print.